MW00885303

Dennis Collins

This book belongs to

_____

happy Hummingbirds

by Dennis Collins

Tate Publishing & Enterprises

Happy Hummingbirds
Copyright © 2008 by Dennis Collins. All rights reserved.

This title is also available as a Tate Out Loud product. Visit www.tatepublishing.com for more information.

No part of this publication may be reproduced, stored in a retrieval system or transmitted in any way by any means, electronic, mechanical, photocopy, recording or otherwise without the prior permission of the author except as provided by USA copyright law.

The opinions expressed by the author are not necessarily those of Tate Publishing, LLC.

Published by Tate Publishing & Enterprises, LLC
127 E. Trade Center Terrace | Mustang, Oklahoma 73064 USA
1.888.361.9473 | www.tatepublishing.com

Tate Publishing is committed to excellence in the publishing industry. The company reflects the philosophy established by the founders, based on Psalm 68:11,
"The Lord gave the word and great was the company of those who published it."

Book design copyright © 2008 by Tate Publishing, LLC. All rights reserved.
Cover design by Janae J. Glass
Interior design by Stephanie Woloszyn
Illustration by Marc Lent

Published in the United States of America

ISBN: 978-1-60604-277-9
1. Juvenile Fiction: General: Animals: Ages 4-7
08.03.28

Hungry hummingbirds hovered around the flower garden. Helen Hummingbird said that she was very thirsty by humming her thirsty tune around the backyard outdoor water faucet.

Howard filled the new hummingbird water feeder with red pomegranate juice and warmed dissolved sugar water. Helen Hummingbird took ten sips from the new water feeder. That recovered her from being too hot on the dry Fourth of July day.

Nine more hummingbirds rushed over to sip from the fancy new hummingbird water feeder. Then back to work in the yard they went, sucking nectar out of each and every flower available. Sweet nectar is the key to the hummingbird's strength and vitality. Soon the sun set.

In the evening the hummingbirds nested for the night in a thick leafy bush. Suddenly a fireworks rocket glided down from the sky and landed in the bush with a small puff of smoke.

All ten hummingbirds stared at the strange rocket. "What are we supposed to do with this?" the hummingbirds thought. Helen Hummingbird began to think. "I know! We will make a bird house out of this strange rocket!" All the birds were amazed by this great idea.

The bottom of the rocket had already burned off completely. The hummingbirds' new rocket home sat sideways in the bush. The rocket had a five-inch opening, so all the birds had to do was hop on in. So they hopped inside the rocket.

"Wow! It echoes in here," Helen Hummingbird noticed. Nest material was piling up very quickly—grass, leaves, and all sorts of tiny debris. Some of the nest material was left in the rocket cone tip for extra warmth.

Howard walks by the new rocket cone nest, not even seeing it. It appears that Howard is too busy cutting a batch of flowers; after all, it does say "Howard's Flower Delivery" on the faded orange-colored vintage panel truck.

Every morning Howard sets his banjo on the front seat of his delivery truck. Often Howard misses playing his banjo in the flower field. He likes to play bluegrass music early in the morning. The hummingbirds like to hear the unusual banjo sound, too. Howard has a really long beard that sometimes gets tangled into his banjo strings!

He gathers five dozen bundles of different flowers to sell today. You can always hear Howard hum as all of the flowers get loaded into his vintage panel truck. "Hum...Hmm... Hmm."

"Hum...Hmm...Hmm."

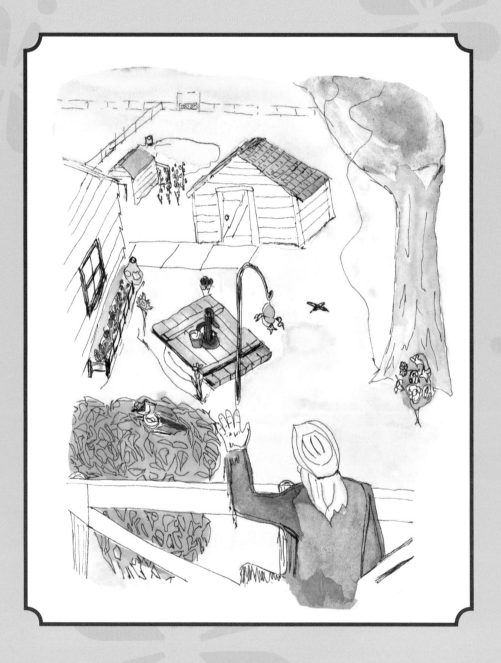

As Howard leaves for work, he waves goodbye to his family, his neighbors, and the hummingbirds. Another day, another dollar, while the hummingbirds are busy again sipping sweet nectar!

The End

listen|imagine|view|experience

AUDIO BOOK DOWNLOAD INCLUDED WITH THIS BOOK!

In your hands you hold a complete digital entertainment package. Besides purchasing the paper version of this book, this book includes a free download of the audio version of this book. Simply use the code listed below when visiting our website. Once downloaded to your computer, you can listen to the book through your computer's speakers, burn it to an audio CD or save the file to your portable music device (such as Apple's popular iPod) and listen on the go!

How to get your free audio book digital download:

1. Visit www.tatepublishing.com and click on the e|LIVE logo on the home page.
2. Enter the following coupon code: 7cdd-0255-7897-aa54-df13-8688-373f-caf5
3. Download the audio book from your e|LIVE digital locker and begin enjoying your new digital entertainment package today!